Dedicated to all special
needs animals waiting for
their forever homes.

#adoptdontshop

ISBN: 978-0-5788729–8-8 Paperback
What Would Lula Do?
www.whatwouldlulado.com

Author: Ginger Cooper
Illustrator: Jessica Zuniga

First printing: April 2021

What would Lula Do?

Inspiration from a Blind Cat

~

Written By Ginger Cooper
Illustrated By Jessica Zuniga

Be fearless.
Know no limits.

Reach for
the flies.

practice self-care

be prepared

Climb every
cat tree
to the top!

Then higher!

And higher!

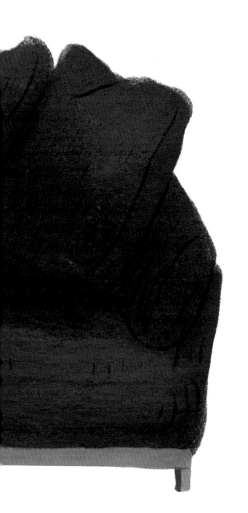

Claim your space!

Find happiness in the coziest of blankets.

Don't let obstacles
get in your way.

When in doubt,
nap it out.

Embrace the
unknown.

Conquer
fear

Curiousity didn't
kill the cat.

Happiness is a
way of life.

Climb
that
table.

Scale
those
stairs.

Swing like a
monkey like
you just
don't
care.

Naps make
everything
better.

Own it.

Be a fearless
warrior princess.

Tackle confrontation head on.

Make kitties
like you.

(Make friends even
if you have to
force them.)

Always, always
be queen of
the mountain.

Don't air your
dirty laundry.

Don't let minor annoyances get in the way of your happiness.

Be flexible,
roll with the punches,
adapt to change.

Laughter is
the best medicine.

Get outside!
Nature is food
for the soul.

Enjoy the
little things.

Meditate daily.

Embrace
new experiences.

Be brave.
Be fearless.
Be Lula.

About Lula

~

(9 / 2009 — 10 / 2020)

Lula was a real life blind kitty who lived with her mom Ginger since she was 12 weeks old. Lula means "famous warrior" and she truly was just that. Lula embraced life with all 4 paws and her tail, loving and living life with gusto. Her blindness was never an issue for her, and her mom lived by the motto "What would Lula do." Lula had courage, joy, gratitude and a goofy personality. She was always ready to play, snuggle, or meditate and loved new experiences.
May we all live even a fraction of our lives like Lula did hers, embracing it with 4 paws and a tail.

 @lulablindkitty